Lewis Halsey

The Falls of Taughannock

Containing a complete description of this the highest fall in the state of

New York : with historical and descriptive sketches

Lewis Halsey

The Falls of Taughannock
Containing a complete description of this the highest fall in the state of New York :
with historical and descriptive sketches

ISBN/EAN: 9783337400699

Printed in Europe, USA, Canada, Australia, Japan

Cover: Foto ©Andreas Hilbeck / pixelio.de

More available books at **www.hansebooks.com**

THE

FALLS OF TAUGHANNOCK:

CONTAINING A

COMPLETE DESCRIPTION

OF THIS THE

Highest Fall in the State of New-York.

WITH HISTORICAL AND DESCRIPTIVE SKETCHES.

BY

LEWIS HALSEY.

ILLUSTRATED BY VIEWS OF THE FALLS.

NEW-YORK:
JOHN A. GRAY & GREEN, PRINTERS, 16 AND 18 JACOB STREET.
MDCCCLXVI.

TO

WILLIAM H. GOODWIN, D.D.,

REGENT OF THE UNIVERSITY OF THE STATE OF NEW-YORK,

THIS LITTLE VOLUME

Is Respectfully Inscribed.

MAY IT RECALL FOR HIM MANY PLEASANT MEMORIES OF BOYHOOD!

INDEX.

INDEX.

PREFACE.

THE want of a description of and guide to the most lofty of the many cataracts of the State of New-York, and one of the most beautiful waterfalls in the world, has been felt by all who have ever visited Taughannock.

This want the present publication aims to supply.

If this Tribute to Taughannock shall be deemed an offering worthy of the theme by those to whom the Falls are familiar, and shall be the means of making this favored spot better known to the lovers of beautiful scenery, the design of the author will be accomplished.

TAUGHANNOCK.

To the true lover of Nature, no spot is more attractive, no landscape more beautiful, than that adorned by her bountiful hand with waterfalls, and wild ravines, and stately forests.

Unlike other and less favored landscapes, that which adds to its attractions the music and brilliancy of cascades and cataracts is ever unfolding new beauties. But when a waterfall, whose vast height adds sublimity to its beauty, grand and gloomy gorges, and picturesque views of lake scenery unsurpassed outside of Switzerland, each, at the same time, present their peculiar attractions, the admiring traveler, delighted by the beauty and awed by the sublimity of the landscape, realizes that he has discovered one of the most favored haunts of nature.

Such is the wild and varied scenery which turns

the attention of the traveler to Taughannock, and, as the fame of the fall spreads abroad, attracts each year a greater throng of visitors.

Rich in romantic glens, charming lakes, and magnificent cataracts, the Empire State may well be called the Switzerland of America. The most lofty, and, in many respects, the most beautiful of her cataracts is Taughannock, situated on a small stream in Tompkins County, three fourths of a mile from Cayuga Lake, and ten miles from Ithaca.

The stream, known as Halsey Creek* from the name of one of the first settlers upon its banks, is one of the largest of the watercourses which intersect the fertile farming lands lying between the twin lakes Cayuga and Seneca. Taking its rise in the highlands midway between them, it flows in an easterly course until at length it unites its waters with those of the calm Cayuga.

Flowing with a gradual and gentle descent through a rich and flourishing country, its banks are dotted with numerous mills and manufacturing establishments.

---

* In our atlases and geographies we find the name thus given, but the stream should have the same name as the fall.

At the distance of a mile and a half from the
lake it would appear that nature had determined to
check the stream in its further progress by erecting
an impassable barrier. This is a rocky ledge, rising
some fifty or sixty feet directly in the path of the
little river. But the stream, by long continued
labor, beginning, perhaps, when darkness was yet
upon the face of the deep, has succeeded in excavat-
ing an enormous channel, from one hundred to four
hundred feet in depth, and four hundred feet across
at its lower extremity. Through this yawning
chasm the victorious waters course triumphantly
onward toward their goal beyond.

This vast gorge, with its frowning cliffs and
towering walls of granite, their grimness relieved
here and there by a bouquet of evergreens, forms the
ravine of Taughannock.

Half a mile after entering this gorge, on account
of a difference in the structure of the rock, while
the height of the banks remain undiminished, the
stream falls perpendicularly two hundred and fifteen
feet into a rocky basin, thus forming a cataract more
than fifty feet higher than Niagara.

The rock over which the water plunges projects
in the center and is contracted on either side, form-

ing a triangle which measures some ninety feet across.

The following jocular but nearly accurate description of Taughannock was published, several years ago, in "Gleason's Pictorial," a Boston magazine:

" It lies about (I like to be particular)
  One mile from Lake Cayuga's western shore,
On either side the rocks rise perpendicular
  Three hundred ninety feet and something more ;
And all the stream, diffused in drops orbicular,
  Descends in clouds and falling mists that pour
Two hundred feet and ten, or nearly so,
Before they form again the stream below."

The following eloquent description of the ravine and falls was written by the celebrated author and orator, George B. Cheever, who visited them in 1859:

GEORGE B. CHEEVER'S DESCRIPTION.

" The Staubbach of Trumansburgh is worth going a great distance to see.

" It is nearly a third higher than any other cataract in our State.

" At present it is the very perfection of beauty,

while the natural mountain gorge, midway in the
progress of which it tumbles over the crags, is one
of the grandest and most picturesque in the world
out of Switzerland. It reminded me much of the
lovely and romantic pass above Chiavenna, in the
Italian Alps. The gorge is at least four hundred
feet in depth, the mountain sides rising jagged and
perpendicular, though with the green forests here
and there clinging to their faces, trees apparently
rooted in the rocks without a particle of soil to
nourish them, and declivities covered with luxuriant
wild shrubbery from the top to the bottom of the
gulf. Here and there the mighty crags advance
half-way across the ravine, round and perfect as
battlemented castles or solid piers, that at some
distant age might have supported a stupendous
natural bridge. At the bottom of the ravine and
at the foot of the fall, looking up the great height,
and watching the extremely graceful and beautiful
descent of the spray, (for the water begins to break
into spray almost at the moment when it begins its
plunge over the precipice,) you feel that nowhere
in the world can it be possible that a more perfectly
beautiful waterfall can be in existence.

"The jagged rock rift, through which the river

rolls before it makes the plunge, is some two hundred feet in depth, the rocky channel becoming a triangle at the brink, and the water plunges some two hundred and twenty feet more to the bottom, where the ravine is upwards of four hundred feet perpendicular. The fall is, in truth, the Staubach of Switzerland most absolutely reproduced, and of concentrated beauty and grandeur.

" When the stream is swollen almost to the utmost capacity of the channel by autumnal rains, or a spring freshet, the beauty of the cataract changes into overwhelming sublimity. It is clothed with the majesty, grandeur, and thunder of Niagara.

" At present you miss the roar, the voice, the sound of many waters, the thunder shaking the earth ; because the volume of water is not deep enough to preserve itself consolidated down the dizzy height of a plunge so tremendous. The coquetting air takes the cataract by its curls on the very forehead of the crags, and tosses and frays it into millions of tiny, fleecy jets, and tangled, shin-ing threads of diamonds and dewy light.

" Each drop gives way to the temptation of a separate display, and with white wings, as of a thousand doves or albatrosses, the vision lights

softly at the bottom of the gorge, with no more
noise than the wind makes when it stirs the leaves
of a mighty forest.

" But when the volume of water is deep enough
in its grand and gloomy channel, all this by-play of
its forces is constrained and concentrated in a unity
of purpose and of plunge, and it rages and roars
down in unceasing thunder as well as eternal foam.
The sublimity then is almost terrific."

LOWER RAVINE.

To obtain the best view of the falls, it is neces-
sary to descend to the bed of the ravine, and follow it upward until we stand at the foot of the
majestic column of water, which towers two hundred feet above us. The wearisome descent of the
steep stairway is forgotten in the enjoyment of the
grand and beautiful scenery with which we are
there surrounded.

Leaving the Taughannock House, (which will be
described hereafter,) we follow a path winding along
the bank of the ravine until we arrive at a long,
steep, and crooked flight of steps. This was built
by the present proprietor of the Taughannock

House, in 1859, and is soon to be replaced by another and more substantial staircase.

Clambering downward, remarking as we descend the course of a landslide which swept away a portion of the steps, we at length arrive at the bottom of the ravine.

Here we find ourselves entering, apparently, the atmosphere of another climate. The ravine, although from two hundred to four hundred feet in width, is shut in by walls so lofty that, except at midday, a large portion of its bed is untouched by the rays of the sun. The air, delightfully cool, fragrant with the perfume of wild roses, and vocal with the music of sweetly murmuring waters, seems to instill new life and vigor into our veins. Venerable forest-trees overshadow us with their rich and variegated foliage, and tower upward in a vain endeavor to catch a glimpse of the rising and setting sun. Creeping vines twine luxuriantly around and above us. Brilliant flowers and handsome mosses are seen on every side. By a winding path, we advance toward the Great Fall, now, for a moment, threading the thick mazes of the overshadowing forest of evergreens; now, as we pass an opening, delaying to gaze upward at the Lilipu-

tian specimens of humanity on the bank above,
unable to recognize them as our friends who are
watching our onward progress; now, reposing beneath the sheltering branches, seated upon the fall-
en trunk of a forest tree. From time to time, we
cross, on rustic bridges, the stream which meanders
through the charming ravine as if conscious of its
beauties, and unwilling to bid them a final farewell.
At length a sudden curve in the banks brings us
unexpectedly in full view of the Great Fall. Here
the chasm widens, and the more lofty walls form a
spacious amphitheatre. On either side the granite
masses tower majestically upward, and seem to
shut us in by an impassable barrier. Before us,
from the frowning cliff hundreds of feet in height,
the mad waters take their terrible leap. The
mighty white column seems clothed with awe-in-
spiring grandeur. The water as it approaches the
edge of the fall is of a deep green color; as soon
as it leavesthe edge it spangles into a thousand
transparent shapes, then, mixing and commingling,
it is dashed into clouds of snowy foam, and descends mists to the depths below.

We never became wearied with gazing upon the
grand and beautiful picture which looms up so

majestically before us. We are continually discovering new attractions. We clamber up the
steep bank to view the picture from another stand-
point. Now we decide in favor of a perspective
view; now we advance, through a storm of misty
rain, to the very face of the fall. Everywhere we
are delighted. Everywhere we are impressed by
the beauty and sublimity of the scene before us.

We recall Byron's unrivaled description of Ve-
lino :

" The roar of waters !—from the headlong height
   [Taughannock] cleaves the wave-worn precipice ;
 The fall of waters ! rapid as the light
   The flashing mass foams, shaking the abyss ;
 The hell of waters ! where they howl and hiss,
   And boil in endless torture ; while the sweat
 Of their great agony, wrung out from this
   Their Phlegethon, curled round the rocks of jet
   That gird the gulf around, in pitiless horror set,

"And mounts in spray the skies, and thence again
   Returns in an unceasing shower, which round,
 With its unemptied cloud of gentle rain,
   Is an eternal April to the ground,
 Making it all one emerald :—how profound
   The gulf ! and how the giant element

From rock to rock leaps with delirious bound,
   Crushing the cliffs, which downward worn and rent
   With his fierce footsteps, yield in chasms a fearful rent."

THE RAINBOW.

"Here," writes a visitor, "we saw distinctly the prismatic colors of the rainbow, mingled with the agitated and gold-green waters."

POOL BELOW THE FALL.

Below the fall, and flowing to the foot of the perpendicular rocks on the right, is a dark pool, perhaps an hundred feet across, and from twenty-five to forty feet in depth.

Large masses of rock are frequently dislodged from the lofty banks, by the action of the winter frost or summer rain, and thunder downward to the ravine below.

THE LADY OF THE MIST.

On the right (or north) of the fall may be seen, when the water is low, a wonderful specimen of Nature's handiwork. It is the apparent represent-ation in the rock of a female, in a half sitting, half reclining posture, one hand resting on the rock by her side, while with the other she withdraws her drapery from contact with the mist and spray. Upon her head is an Egyptian head-dress,* or, as it sometimes appears, a helmet, resembling those seen in ancient pictures of Minerva.

This wonderful conformation in the rocks was first noticed in 1865, by Colonel T. A. Merriman, of Auburn. The remarkably distinct outlines of the figure can be easily traced by the visitor standing a fourth of a mile away on the bank in front of the Taughannock House.

THE GOTHIC DOOR.

Towering far upward on the right of the fall is a deep indentation in the rocks, bearing a striking resemblance to a gigantic Gothic door, its lofty arch rising higher than even the fall itself. This singular formation is alluded to in the beautiful poem by Mr. Parker:

"I love to think that in thy rocky walls,
    Where stands the strangely perfect Gothic Door,

---

* "Such as are seen on the numerous bas-reliefs in the catacombs, and among the ruins of Egypt."

The genii have reared their magic halls,
  With crystal column and with pearly floor."

On account of the frequent changes, produced
by the crumbling away of the rocks, the Gothic
door has lost much of its symmetry and beauty,
but the resemblance is still easily traceable.

The following extract is from the correspondence
of the *New-York Observer*.

MR. WELCH'S ACCOUNT.

" But there is a feature of the lake scenery yet in
store for us, surpassing any thing that we have seen,
alas, too often unknown to the tourist, and therefore
passed by unnoticed, which would itself repay the
traveler for a journey across the State, if there were
nothing else worth seeing along the entire way. I
refer to Taughannock Falls, ten miles below the head
of the lake.

" The steamboat landing is unpretentious and by
no means attractive; but the number that land there
is steadily increasing, and will continue to hereafter,
as it becomes better known, until the accommodations shall become the best on the lake.

" A few rods from the shore, and quite out of sight

from the steamer, the tourist is suddenly confronted by the mouth of a grand gorge, three hundred feet deep, perhaps one third as broad—between perpendicular walls of solid rock, with a waterfall pouring down its rocky bed. This gorge extends back for a mile, deepening and widening into the heart of the mountain with fantastic curves and overhanging cliffs, and a frontlet of pines on either brow. The adventurous pedestrian may thread the entire gorge with, perhaps, the single risk of wet feet as he passes from island to island on the way.

"Before he reaches the second or grand fall, he will observe an almost perpendicular ladder of more than two hundred steps, ascending to the summit of the cliff. If he decline to thread the entire length of the ravine, he may make the circuit of the public road, the side of which borders the brink of the gorge, permitting him to trace its windings as he proceeds, and look down into its dizzy depths.

"Then he can descend from the road by the perpendicular ladder to the bottom of the ravine on his way to the second fall. The gorge swells upward and around him into a magnificent amphitheatre, echoing and reëchoing with the noise of the distant rapid and fall. Suddenly there breaks upon his view a cataract, making a single leap of two hundred and fifty feet from a pathway sixty feet wide and a hundred feet deep, which it has cut through the solid rock. Sometimes, when the gorge is filled with water, it is a raging cataract, shaking the firm hills with its thunder. Now, when the stream is low, it forms one of the most beautiful cascades that any land can boast. It resembles the Dust-Falls of Staubbach, which is the pride of Switzerland; though inferior in height, yet it is superior to it in some other respects; its waters are nearer milky white, the height is not so great as to dash it completely to dew-dust in its fall; it has just water enough to retain some consistency, and yet descent enough to make it thin, and light, and soft, as a pendent vail of snowy gauze, with which the air is fondly sporting and which occasional gusts from below lift into successive graceful snowy folds, inwrought with colors of the rainbow, which float awhile before the eye ere they sink into the seething lakelet that circles below. No words, however, can convey a just idea of the commingled beauty of cascade, precipice, cliff, and gorge; the pencil has made the attempt, but, in the sketches I have seen, has sadly failed to do it justice.

"Opposite the fall stands the Taughannock house, for the accommodation of visitors. From either story of the house the fall is visible, through the leafy trees. The easy swing and rustic seats are each arranged to command a peculiar view. The perfume of pine fills the air with healthy fragrance, and its whispering music floats upon the breeze. Unpretentious but most satisfactory entertainment cheers the visitor, and prepares him for an after-dinner stroll to the third falls or succession of charming cascades, eighty rods beyond, which should by no means be neglected, for these alone are sufficient to repay one's delay at Taughannock.

"My only regret was that I must bid adieu so soon to the lovely scene. It was, however, with the firm resolve that whenever I might enjoy a sail over Cayuga Lake, I would not pass Taughannock by."

THE HERMIT.

In the summer of 1826, there appeared in the village of Trumansburgh a stranger. None knew, or could learn, who he was or whence he came. His whole history was shrouded in obscurity. The story of his former life he never told ; and even his name and home remained concealed.

Seeking no associates, inviting no confidences, and seeming ever to avoid the society of men, the curiosity of the villagers suffered no abatement concerning him.   To them he was an unsolved enigma.

In a short time, however, the stranger disappeared, and for several days was unheard from; but, on account of his eccentric habits, little notice was taken of his departure.

A few days passed by, when a lad, wandering in the ravine of Taughannock, discovered the mangled body of the recluse, lying near the water, a short distance below the fall.

His death was as mysterious as had been his life. None ever knew, whether, attracted by the fascinating beauty of the cataract, he had ventured too far and fallen a victim to his rashness, or whether, weary of life, he had madly cast himself into this horrible abyss.

By stranger hands the body of the poor unfortunate was buried, and no friend came to weep over his grave.   He had lived unknown and unloved—he died unmourned.

Such was the sad, mysterious fate of the NAMELESS HERMIT OF TAUGHANNOCK.

CAVES.

Not far from the mouth of the ravine, and halfway up the north bank, are three small caves, in length from forty to one hundred and fifty feet.

They, with several others which have since been filled up, were excavated, some thirty years ago, by a superannuated Methodist minister, Richard Goodwin by name, who worked them with the expectation of discovering a vein of coal.

Although not extensive, these caves must have required in their formation severe and long-continued labor.

Comical stories are told of this curious old Rip Van Winkle of the neighborhood, who, regardless of the sneers of his neighbors and the disappointment resulting from his long and fruitless labors, still perseveringly and dogmatically grubbed away at the rock, even, as is said, to the day of his death.

Once, and only once, was the old man blessed with the belief that his weary labors were about to be crowned with success, and even then he was doomed to experience a sad disappointment; for some mischievous boys had placed a few lumps of coal in one of his caves, hoping thus to excite his expectations and stimulate him to future exertions.

The upper and largest cave is the only one now visited, and even this is partially filled up at its entrance. When once inside the explorer is barely able to walk upright, and discovers the damp walls hung with bats, who are seldom disturbed by other visitors.

In the ravine below, and not far from these caves, are two small sulphur springs.

FIGHT WITH A BEAR AT TAUGHANNOCK.

The following simple yet graphic account of a fight with a bear in the ravine of Taughannock, was contributed by Mr. George Weyburn to the "New-York State Historical Collections," published by John M. Barber and Henry Howe in 1844.

It is amusing to note what importance this old veteran gives to the least incident of this great "conflict," which he describes with as much zeal and earnestness as if he were discoursing concerning a Waterloo, upon the issue of which the destinies of the world were depending.

His enumeration of the numbers, positions, and arms of the combatants is worthy of a careful chroniclcr, and he is unable to conceal his joy when, after recommencing "the conflict," his friends are at length left "masters of the field."

"One Sunday evening in October, about forty-seven years ago, as my father, Mr. Samuel Weyburn, was returning from feeding his horse on the north side of the creek, near where the distillery now stands, his dog started up a bear and her two cubs. They followed their course up the hill on the south side of the creek until near the summit, a few rods above the mill-site fall, where the cubs took to a tree. My father ran to the house, and, having obtained his gun, pursued. Being directed by the barking of the dog, he passed about twenty rods beyond the tree in which the cubs were, and there he found the bear with her back against a tree, standing on the brink of a gulf, defending herself from the attacks of the dog.

"He fired, and, as it was afterward found, broke one of her fore-legs. The animal retreated into the gulf, and was seen no more that night.

"In the mean time my mother, brother, and myself, who had followed in the pursuit, came to the tree in which the cubs had retreated, who, being frightened at the report of the gun and the sound of our voices, began to cry '*mam! mam!*' in the most affecting tones, strongly resembling the human voice.

"My mother having called my father, he shot the cubs and returned home. The next morning, my father thinking that he had either killed or severely wounded the animal, for the want of a better weapon, (having expended his only charge of powder the evening previous,) took a pitchfork, and proceeded in quest of the enemy, accompanied by myself and brother.

"I was armed with a small ax; but my brother, not being equipped for war, was allowed to accompany us bare-handed.

"Thus accoutered and followed by our dog, we proceeded to within about forty rods of the great fall, when my father, apprised of the nearness of the enemy by the barking of the dog, ran and left us in the rear.

"We soon came in sight of the bear and dog, who were passing from the left wall of the precipice across the basin to the right, and ascended almost to the perpendicular rock, a distance of eighty or one hundred feet.

"My father, climbing up lower down, was enabled to intercept her passage in consequence of her broken limb.

"Here the action again commenced by his giving her three thrusts with the fork. The first and second were near the heart, the third struck her shoulder-blade, when she turned upon him, and he met her with a thrust in her face, putting out one of her eyes with one prong and tearing her tongue with the other. She then rushed toward him, his feet gave way, and as he fell she caught him by the clothes near his breast.

" At this juncture he seized her and threw her below him. This he repeated two or three times in their descent toward the bottom of the ravine, during which she bit him in both his legs and in his arms. At the bottom, in the creek, lay a stone whose front was not unlike the front of a common cooking-stove, the water reaching to the top. Near this, four or five feet distant, stood a rock on the bank. Into this snug notch it was his good luck to throw his antagonist, with her feet and claws toward the rock in the stream. In this situation he succeeded in holding her, with his back to hers and braced between the rocks. With his left hand he held her by the back, and with his right held her by the neck, until I came up.

I struck her with all my might on the back with the ax. At this my father sprang from her and seized his fork. The bear turned toward us with a shake and a snort. I gave her a severe blow. She fell, but, recovering herself, endeavored to retreat. We recommenced the conflict, and ere long the lifeless corpse of the animal proclaimed us masters of the field.

The victory was dearly bought. The blood was running in streams from my father's hands, and from his limbs into his shoes.

On examination, he found that she had bitten him in each limb, inflicting four ugly wounds at each bite, besides a slit in his wrist, supposed to have been done by one of her claws.

DURING HIGH WATER.

The scene is then one of surpassing grandeur.

The rivulet of July or August, which murmured so musically along within its narrow channel, becomes the tempestuous torrent, overwhelming with resistless might all which would obstruct its path.

Like some wild and ferocious animal, which has

2

been tamed and reduced to servitude by the power of man, but now, frightened or enraged, he has become forgetful of all his former lessons, and, threatening with destruction all who endeavor to approach him, riots unrestrained. Thus this little river, once a wild and ungoverned torrent, but since introduced by man into new channels, compelled to grind his grain, saw his lumber, press out his oil and wine, and make his paper; now, rising in sudden and fierce rebellion against him, has broken over the boundaries which he had placed, resumed its ancient channel, and, having thus escaped from his hated dominion, rushes exultingly onward, breaking or bearing along with it the chains with which he has sought to impede its progress.

The beautiful little cascade of summer, floating downward, as if on fairy wings, to the deep ravine below, tinkling upon the rocks with music like that which breathes from Æolian harps, half-hiding the granite wall with a vail of misty whiteness, its waters bright and pure, and clear as crystal, which, after falling, glides gently and noiselessly away to the bosom of the lake beyond; this we behold no more.

The scene is wonderfully changed; and were it not for the eternal rocks, we could imagine that another landscape was stretched out before us.

The rushing river, unrestrained by its narrow channel, has swept away the rustic bridges, and overflowed the winding paths by which we ascend to the foot of the fall.

> " Lo ! where it comes like an eternity,
>   As if to sweep down all things in its track,
>   Charming the eye with dread—a matchless cataract."

The ravine is filled with the sound of rushing floods.

The majestic column of water swells into grander proportions, while the voice of the cataract, growing hoarser and more terrible, seems striving to rival the roar of the mighty Niagara.

WINTER BEAUTIES.

In many respects the winter beauties of Taughannock surpass those of summer, although each season has its peculiar attractions.

In summer, the scene is one of unequaled beauty; in winter, one of surpassing grandeur.

A huge mass of ice, its base stretching out one

hundred feet from the foot of the fall, and sometimes rising to the height of an hundred and fifty
feet, towers upward like some mighty temple. Immense ice-pendants from above join the ice-moun-
tain below, and form an appropriate tower to the
crystal cathedral.   Monstrous icicles, stretching
downward on all sides of the ravine, almost conceal its sombre walls.

When the sun, piercing the wintry clouds, lights
up this mountain and these towering walls of ice,
tinging their tops with crimson and gold, one can
almost imagine that he beholds the magical palace
of Aladdin, with gorgeous towers, and shining bat-
tlements, and crystal columns crowned with gold.

BREAKING UP OF THE ICE.

The breaking up of the ice in the spring affords
another spectacle of grandeur and beauty.

The water, gaining volume, falls farther forward
than before, and dashes its weight against the
mountain of ice below. This mass is gradually
worn away, and immense fissures are opened,
through which the foaming and angry waters can
be seen struggling to escape from their prison.

Now a huge mass of ice lunges slowly forward,

and is hurled over the precipice with a report
which makes the surrounding hills reverberate.
Now a succession of smaller fragments sends up
sounds like the discharge of a park of artillery;
and, as the finer particles come rushing after, the
listener can imagine that he hears the rattle of
musketry intermingled with the roar of heavy
ordnance.

PICTURES OF TAUGHANNOCK.

Excellent photographic and stereoscopic pictures
of scenery about Taughannock have been obtained
by Dr. J. Towler, of Hobart College, by Messrs.
Tolles and Seely, of Ithaca, and other skillful
artists.

Messrs. Tolles and Seely have some beautiful
views of the Falls and Ravine, which can scarcely
be surpassed.

THE TAUGHANNOCK HOUSE.

The Taughannock House, a substantial and spacious wooden building, stands in a pleasant grove a
short distance below the falls. Here the traveler
always finds excellent accommodations and an oblig-
ing landlord.

This pleasant hotel has recently been enlarged

to double its former size and refurnished, and, under the management of its present popular proprietor, will continue to deserve and receive the
patronage of the public.

Immediately in front of the Taughannock House
is the point referred to elsewhere for obtaining the
best view of both ravine and fall. From the second and third stories of the Hotel, the falls may
be indistinctly seen, half-concealed by the waving
branches of the trees.

THE SPRING.

A little to the right is a deep notch in the ravine
bank, where a flight of steps leads down to a cool,
sparkling spring, unfailing even in seasons of the
greatest drought. Here a large grape-vine, running along the very brink of the precipice, serves
as a protection to the visitor who wishes to peep
over the edge of the bank.

The following extract is from a pamphlet, descriptive of Cayuga Lake and the scenery along
its banks, published by Munsell & Rowland, Al-
bany, 1860 :

"TAGHCANIC FALLS.

The traveler who does not stop here denies him-

self the pleasure of seeing the most beautiful waterfall in the State. At a point about one mile up a
wild but accessible ravine, the clear crystal stream
pours over a shelf of rock in an unbroken, exqui-
site vail of water — the great distance (over two
hundred feet) of its plunge, changing it to the
dreamiest and most delicious cloud-work of spray.
These falls have met delighted description from the
skilled pens of Dr. Cheever, Mrs. Ellet, and many
others who have not omitted to see this sweet sister
of Niagara. There is just enough water; more
would change the dream-like character of this silver vail hung in a great deep glen. At the

TAGHCANIC HOTEL,

kept by Mr. Halsey, will be found admirable ar-
rangements of entertainment. It is of the best
grade of hotels, and will be found to deserve this
word of commendation."

VIEW OF CAYUGA LAKE.

A pleasant path, through the woods fragrant
with the breath of the pines, leads us a short distance below the Taughannock House, where, from a
rustic seat agreeably situated in a shady nook, we

obtain a beautiful view of Cayuga Lake, recalling some of the most charming landscapes on the Hudson. This is a picture which must be seen to be appreciated by the tourist, as no description of ours can do it justice. On either hand extend the bright shores, spotted with field and forest, while here and there arises the single spire of a little hamlet.

Far away to the north is seen Marsh's Point,* a favorite resort for summer excursionists, and on the opposite shore, as if to extend friendly greeting, another long and slender point reaches out a sparkling finger.

Between these pleasant shores stretches the silver surface of Cayuga — queen of five sister lakes, a glittering gem, set in a landscape only to be appreciated by the true artist. Here and there appears a snowy sail, or a little steamer puffing sluggishly along, with a cloud of black smoke following in her wake.

For twenty miles or more, we can watch the shining wavelets circling with beauty the rocky bluffs, green meadows, and glittering headlands,

---

* We would direct attention to beautiful views of Marsh's Point and surrounding scenery photographed by Messrs. Tolles and Seely.

until, in the dim distance, the waters are mingled with the sky.

DEATH OF THE HORSE.

A short distance below the hotel, an accident occurred in 1865, which happily resulted in nothing more serious than the loss of a horse and buggy. The animal, becoming frightened or fractious, began to back toward the precipice. The driver had only time to disengage himself from the reins, in which he had become entangled, when horse and wagon together tumbled down the steep declivity to where the rocks rise perpendicular; then their fall was unbroken until they were dashed upon the rocks hundreds of feet below and crushed into innumerable fragments.

Strange to relate, however, a violin, which was in the buggy, was preserved from harm by its case, and was recovered uninjured.

The scattered fragments of the horse were collected and buried in the bed of the stream, where head and foot-stones were erected to mark his grave. Few of our cemeteries are more beautiful than the spot where the departed steed lies sleeping. The swiftly gliding waters murmur music above him;

from neighboring groves Æolian harps mingle their strains with the melody, while the fragrance of wild flowers perfumes the air around.

ACCIDENT.

There are two paths leading into the upper ravine, but the traveler will find the second easier in its descent.

Near the first of these paths, and not far from the fall itself, an accident occurred in the summer of 1865. An Irishman, who visited the falls with a picnic party, in attempting to scramble down the bank here, lost his balance, and, by alternate rollings and tumblings, was precipitated to the bottom of the ravine. Here, bruised and almost breathless, he lay during a long and weary night, unable even to drag himself to the water, which was flowing near him. He managed to quench his thirst by dipping a broken branch in the stream and applying the moistened end to his lips. After remaining here for the greater part of the following day, he recovered himself sufficiently to crawl up the bank and to the Cataract House, where, exhausted and fainting, he was received and cared for.

UPPER RAVINE.

The upper ravine, although its banks are less majestic, surpasses the lower in rustic beauty. Descending the bank by an easy, winding path, our curiosity is aroused and our admiration excited by the wonderfully regular appearance of several smooth, deep hollows in the rock which constitutes the bed of the stream. These cavities form bowl-like bathing places, round and polished as if hollowed by the hand of art. The largest of these natural bathing-tubs, where the water revolves in a sort of miniature whirlpool, is called the

DEVIL'S PUNCH-BOWL.

We now descend to the brink of the Fall, and, crossing the stream, find ourselves upon TABLE ROCK, so called from its resemblance to the well-known Table Rock at Niagara.

Our rock is a granite platform, immediately to the right of and almost level with the top of the Fall, with a narrow shelf projecting for several yards on the face of the massive wall beyond, along which the most venturesome visitors carry fragments of rock and drop them into the water below.

A. report like that of a rifle rises from the dark abyss.

From this point is obtained a charming view of the lower ravine, the Taughannock House, and the lake in the distance.

Retracing our steps, and passing the Devil's

Punch-Bowl, we meet with one of the numerous pretty little cascades with which the upper ravine abounds. Thence a pleasant path leads us meanderingly onward toward the second or UPPER FALL, near where the stream first cuts its way into the rock.

Here, at a sudden turn, there bursts upon our view a cataract, fifty feet in height, and of peculiar beauty. The water does not fall perpendicularly, but, dashed into foam, leaps madly from rock to rock until, as if ashamed of the efforts of its divided strength, collecting its forces in a narrow channel, it pours its fury upon the rocks below.

On the left of this fall the smooth wall of rock rises in a beautiful curve, as regularly arched as if built by the hand of man.

THE OLD GUN-FACTORY.

A short distance above the second fall, and near the upper entrance to the gorge, stands a dilapidated relic of the war of 1812, known as the "Gun-Factory."

The building was erected in 1814 or 1815, and a company was at that time engaged in manufacturing guns under a Government contract. At the close of the war the company had a large number of guns partially completed, which, as the Government had no use for them, were boxed up and sent to an arsenal in Connecticut.

After the war, the old gun-factory was for a long

time unoccupied, but has since served as an oil-mill, a flax-mill, and a tobacco-house.

MEANS OF ACCESS.

During the summer season, Taughannock is easily accessible from all parts of the country, as a double line of boats on Cayuga Lake connects with the New-York Central at Cayuga Bridge, and with a branch of the New-York and Erie at Ithaca.

The ride over the clear and placid waters of the bright Cayuga affords pleasure enough of itself to repay the traveler for all the expense of his journey·

The steamboat company are now building a new passenger-boat to take the place of one of the old steamers.

In winter Taughannock is more difficult of approach, as for two months Cayuga Lake is closed by ice; but a line of stages from Ovid to Ithaca connects with conveyances from the Seneca Lake boats, thus opening another pleasant way of approach to Taughannock.

These steamers can always be relied upon, both during summer and winter. In 1865, one of them, Captain Dey's boat, did not lose a single trip during the year.

TAUGHANNOCK BY MOONLIGHT.

BY ———.

I ONCE saw Taughannock by moonlight, and shall never forget the impression it made upon me. It forms one of my memory pictures which never can fade away, and which I love frequently, to revert to.

As our carriage rolled along the smooth road skirting the ravine, and we passed now beneath the shadows of dark pines, now over a strip of bright moonlight, I was continually leaning from the windows, watching the constant alternation of light and shade. The wheels bowled along so smoothly it seemed as if we were moved by enchantment. I couldn't help comparing our little company to a group of fairies hastening to a midnight revel in a coach drawn through the air,

> "Over hill, over dale,
> Through bush, through briar,
> Over park, over pale,
> Through flood, through fire."

Surely, never Titania or Oberon sported on a green beneath a more dazzling flood of moonlight.

We whirled around corners, glided in and out, following the windings of the ravine of whose black depths I caught a shuddering glance now and then, until finally the forest closed in on both sides, the rays of the moon struggled in vain to penetrate the thick branches, and we·rode in silence, ascending and descending several slight elevations, halting at last with the quietness that had hitherto characterized our course, at the broad piazza fronting the Cataract House.

The song of the

"Cadenced white waterfall, silvered and curled,"

reached us in subdued utterances, as if the moon had laid a spell upon it, and the voices of the water-spirits were low in consequence. Crossing the open space in front of the hotel, we seated ourselves upon the verge of the ravine, reverently prepared to look and listen. The fall was visible, silvered at the top where the moonlight struck it, and dropping away into shadowy indistinctness ere it reached the stream below. The sigh of the night breeze, mingled with the ceaseless murmur of the

cascade, seemed the only sound awake in the wide
world.   .

Far down the dark abyss beneath us, and away
up into the infinitude above us, we looked, feeling
our littleness.

A still, small voice seemed sounding in our ears
the praises of Him who created the world, reared
its venerable forests, fashioned its wondrous and
beautiful adornings, piled up its mountain heights
heights and scooped out its deep-cut ravines.

At first there was a spell upon every tongue, and
no word was uttered; then we began to talk in
whispers, and, the seal of silence once removed, it
was not long ere there was a mingling of voices
and an interchange of opinion with regard to Taughannock.

" Beautiful ! isn't it ?"

" Heavenly !"

" Divine !"

" Shall we descend and pay Undine a visit ?"

" Where do you suppose her grotto is situated ?"

"Oh ! beneath that cliff yonder, where the water
shoots over and the spray rises."

Undine ! The name called up a host of shadowy
dreams. I saw the doomed maiden floating on the

2*

curling spray, her pale hair unbound, her sad face turned toward us.

Surely, I thought, the spirits that haunt each rippling stream must love to congregate in such a spot on such a night as this.

Misty and indistinct as the waterfall seemed, there was yet enough of it visible to charm and enchain us to the spot for hours.

"*Les trois Sœurs*," with sweet voices and charming faces, sang a duet about "Moonlight, music, love, and flowers," and never was melody more in tune with the harmonies about us.

The sentinel trees ranged along the edge of the ravine stood stately and dark in the full glow of the moon, like sturdy guardians whose vigils might never for an instant relax. When we moved about, the last year's foliage of the pine lay soft and smooth beneath our feet, and its aromatic odors filled the air.

There were strange whisperings overhead, as if the Dryads were interchanging their nightly communications.

I know not how late we might have remained had not an evil spirit prompted some member of the company to look at his watch.

"Eleven o'clock!"

"Impossible!"

With the settled conviction that his watch had beaten old Time by at least a couple of hours, every time-piece in the party was consulted, but alas! each told a similar story. One more look at the silvery sheen of the falling waters, one long and lingering look to imprint the scene upon memory, one moment of eager and intent listening to catch the song those waters are forever singing, and we are driven slowly away with many a backward glance at the quiet hotel with its surroundings of "forest primeval."

VIEWS.

— • • • —

One of the best unobstructed views from the top of the bank, is obtained from the rustic seat immediately in front of the hotel. Here, across the tremendous gulf which yawns before us, we behold the falls in the distance, their mighty walls of granite guarding them on either side. We behold the "Gothic Door," opening grandly, on the right, and the "Lady of the Mist," sitting meditatively near the foot of the fall. This is also a favorable position for viewing the beautiful lower ravine.

From this point was painted one of the best pictures of Taughannock—a large oil painting, by that talented artist, J. C. Beardsley, of Ithaca. Mr. Beardsley excels in landscape painting, and has made many beautiful studies at Taughannock.

A few rods south-west of the Taughannock House, near the spot where once stood another hotel, called the "FALLS HOUSE," we obtain a nearer view of the fall, which is preferred by some to that in front of the Cataract. The prospect of the ravine, however, is more limited, in consequence of its curving suddenly to the left, and it is impossible to appreciate here the height of the bank upon which we are standing. We have a fine view of the pool beneath the fall, and of the towering bank opposite.

A little further up-stream is a steep path, leading downward almost to the edge of the perpendicular wall rising from below. Here the venturesome traveler will discover another beautiful view of the fall. This spot was once the scene of a sad tragedy.

Directly beneath this point was discovered the body of the stranger to whose mournful fate we have alluded elsewhere.

As at Niagara the best points for viewing the falls are found on the Canada shore, so here, as the water falls almost facing the northern bank, it is impossible to obtain a satisfactory view of Taughannock from the southern. There is, however, one view from that side which is worth mentioning. It is obtained by standing near the edge of the overhanging bank, nearly in line with the fall itself, and apparently almost directly above it. This position, however, is not an entirely safe one, as portions of the projecting rock fall every year.

BEAUTIFUL VIEW.

Not far from the top of the fall, and the first path for descending to the stream above, is the best point for obtaining a view of that magnificent gulf, the lower ravine.

We have never seen a painting or a good stereoscopic view of this scene, although several artists have endeavored to obtain one; but we know of no landscape which would make a more beautiful picture, if it could be successfully transferred to canvas. The massive granite walls, on either side, diminishing in the distance; the dark pool, three hundred feet beneath, from which a sparkling cloud of foam arises; the stream below, no longer disturbed by the terrible fright of its fall—a thread of silver winding away among the evergreens; and a bird's-eye view of the beautiful Cayuga in the distance; all these commend this favored spot to the attention of the artist.

These are the most favorable positions from which to survey the cataract and ravine from above.

VIEWS FROM BELOW.

The view of the fall from the ravine, however, is the only one with which we are entirely satisfied. Here alone we are fully impressed with the overpowering sublimity of the scene, and while we can not but admire its beauty, its grandeur fills us with awe.

None of the views from above afford us an adequate idea of the height, breadth, or beauty of the fall, but from below it stands out in all its magnificent proportions, a masterpiece of nature's handiwork, painted upon the face of the mighty rocks, with lofty and overhanging cliffs to mingle in due proportions the lights and shadows.

A near approach to the "Lady of the Mist," confuses to our sight the outlines of her figure, and we discover that in this instance—

"Distance lends enchantment;"

but the Gothic Door rises grand and gloomy above us, like the dilapidated portal of some gigantic castle of the olden time. The pool, which looked so small from above, swells into quite a lakelet, extending a stone's throw from the foot of the fall.

HISTORICAL.

It would be but a pleasant task to retrace the history of Taughannock, through the ages which have passed since first its waters began to flow, to learn at what period, and with what rapidity, it formed, first a succession of rapids, and, finally, this majestic cataract; to know what nations and tribes have in turn dwelt along its banks, and held sway over these pleasant shores.

The beautiful and appropriate name of the Falls, we are well aware, descends to us from the American Indians, and Dr. Hamilton has given us a charming legend of the manner in which the Delaware name, Taughannock, came to be applied to this cataract in the country of the Iroquois, or Six Nations.

But there are many and indubitable evidences that before the time of the Indians, other and more civilized races claimed this country as their own. Mementoes and monuments of a strange unknown people are scattered over our country, from the Atlantic to the Pacific, and from Lake Erie to the Gulf of Mexico; but none can tell their history, or to whom we owe their existence.

Between the Lakes Cayuga and Seneca, and along Lake Erie, were discovered the remains of many of those mysterious, ancient fortifications, belonging to an age so remote that even the tongue of tradition is silent concerning them.

Various theories have been advanced in regard to the origin of these unknown nations of the past, and the time at which they inhabited this country, but it is doubtful whether we shall ever be able to determine accurately concerning either of the points in question.

In later years we know that this beautiful country was the home of the Cayugas and Senecas, the chief tribes of the great Iroquois confederacy, who doubtless built their wigwams along the banks of the Taughannock.

The spot which is now a place of popular resort for the votary of pleasure, was then a favored haunt of the simple child of nature. Where the devotees of fashion "wind 'mid the mazes" of "the Lancers," the painted warriors then brandished their hatchets in the war-dance; and instead of the sweet notes of the lute or viol, floating through the brilliant ball-room, the shrill whoop of the savage rung through the forest.

But the emotions of the heart remain the same, and where now the proud beauty twirls her fan, and listens, with half-concealed contempt, to the familiar tale of another suitor, the modest Indian maiden, her dark cheek tinged with a deeper hue, acknowledged her first and only love.

No doubt the wild " children of the forest "

" Felt awe as deep and reverential love,"

toward the Great Spirit, whose hand they recognized in the works of nature, as do many of their more enlightened pale-faced conquerors, who boast so loudly of their mental and moral superiority.

In no other part of North-America had the aborigines made such advances in civilization as upon the shores of these lakes and in the Genesee country. Those of our readers who have been accustomed to think of the Indians as wild and savage warriors will be astonished to learn how far they had advanced in the arts of peace.*

* Vide Trans. N. Y. State Agricultural Society, Vol. X. 1850, p. 380.

We quote from an authentic account of General Sullivan's expedition against the Indians, in 1779:

" After the battle at Newtown [now Elmira] the American army pressed forward between Cayuga and Seneca lakes, driving the Indians before them.

" Here the lands were found to be cultivated, yielding corn abundantly. Extensive orchards presented fine fruits to the invader. The apple, pear, and plum were abundant. A regularity in the arrangement of their houses indicated long-continued prosperity and enjoyment of property. Many houses were rudely framed, with chimneys, and some few were painted. All, however, were destroyed."

We are informed, by early settlers, that, at the time of the first emigration of the whites into this region of country, there were unmistakable evidences that a large and long-established INDIAN VILLAGE had existed on the point now known as Goodwin's, below Taughannock Falls. At the time of the coming of the whites the village had been abandoned, probably on account of the gradual decimation of the tribes, but the Indians still cultivated corn-fields on this point, and had also an orchard here.

For many years hatchets and other Indian imple-
ments would often be turned up by the plow, and it
was no uncommon thing for laborers in the corn-
fields to discover quantities of the wampum, or
large red beads, used as money by the Indians.

INDIAN ORCHARD.

The Indian apple orchard was near the mouth of
the stream, and some of the trees were standing only
a few years ago.

It was supposed by the settlers that this orchard
was cut down at the time of Gen. Sullivan's expedition in 1779 ; and that new trees sprouted up
from the old stumps. This opinion was strength-
ened by the fact that frequently two or three trees
grew together in a cluster, as if springing from a
common root. These apple-trees grew to an unusual height, and several old settlers bear testimony
that they produced excellent fruit.

A tree from this orchard was once transplanted
by Abner Truman* (the revolutionary soldier from
whom the village of Trumansburgh derives its

---

* The name was originally Tremain. It was corrupted in pronunciation to Truman, hence Trumansburgh.

name) to his garden, opposite the present Methodist church. This venerable tree* has been very productive, and still stands, bearing fruit yearly.

Mr. George Goodwin, of Jacksonville, relates that for a long time after his father settled at "the Point," although the land had been nominally sold to the white men, the Indians claimed the fruit of the orchard as their own. They would even steal the apples before they were ripe, and it was several years before they ceased to be troublesome.

ORIGIN OF NAME.

Before Dr. Hamilton had investigated this subject, many different views were entertained concerning the origin of the name Taughannock.

Various attempts were made to discover in the word itself the reason for its being thus applied.†
But the theories thus advanced, although ingenious, were all open to objections.

Probably there are few words for which a skillful

---

* It is supposed to be nearly one hundred years old.

† Mr. Bogart (vide quotation following) made the word to mean, "The Great Fall in the Woods." Dr. Geo. Copway, the Indian chief, thought it might mean, "The Crevice which rises to the Tops of the Trees."

philologist could not discover some possible derivation.

We give a few names and terminations from which such an investigator might suppose a deriva tion for the name Taughannock :

In the Algonquin, the word *tahuun* means wood ; *olamehukuum*, high ; *patihaakun*, thunder. In the Miami tongue forest is *tawwonawkewe*, in Delaware it is *taikunah*. *Tahxxan*, in Delaware, means wood. In the Dacotah dialect, *tehauwaukan* means very high.

Schoolcraft states that " the tribes generally dwelt on the banks of rivers, which were denoted by an inflection to the root form of its name, as, *-annah*, *-annock*, *-any*, as heard in Susqueh-annah, Rappah-annock, and Allegh-any.

" The termination of *-atun*, or *-atan*, or *-ton*, denotes a rapid stream or channel. In Iroquois, the particle *on* denotes a hill ; *-ock* denotes forest."

The following entry was recently made in the register of the Taughannock House, by W. H. Bogart, Esq., of the New-York "WORLD":

" Mr. Halsey requested Mr. Alfred B. Street, the distinguished poet, and myself, to ascertain what was the probable signification of the word Taghánic, by which these very, very beautiful Falls are designated. Few things are so difficult as to gather from the conflicting dialects of the various tribes any accurate translation.

" Mr. Street will do his portion of the task, set him by Mr. Halsey, in his own delightful manner, by ode or lyric worthy of the theme. I find in a dictionary of the *Onondaga* language, prepared by Jean Murinchau, a French Jesuit, the word *dehennah*, or *dehennach*, meaning, I believe, a Fall. In the Algonquin is the word *taakhan*, which is interpreted as Woods, and in the Mohawk, *tungkah*, the explanation of which is Great. All these brought together are easily, in the changes of language and varieties of pronunciation, rendered as Taghannic, or

THE GREAT FALL IN THE WOODS !

which is the easy, and natural, and probable appellation given to it by the quiet, simple, unimaginative men, who once ruled and possessed all this land.

" WILLIAM H. BOGART.

" AURORA, CAYUGA LAKE,

" 7th August, 1865."

The name Taughannock, like many others of a similar derivation, has been spelled and pronounced in a great variety of ways, and by scarcely two writers in the same way.

After an examination of other Indian geographical terms, and after consulting with gentlemen who have long been familiar with Indian languages and dialects, we have adopted the orthography, *Taughannock*, as most in accordance with the structure of the language from which it is derived, while we believe it to be, also, the best sounding name of all those applied to the Falls. We thus preserve in the word the guttural *augh*, and the termination *annock*, analogous to Rappahannock, etc.

NOTE.—for Indian geographical names, used in this book, compare "The League of the Iroquois," by Lewis H. Morgan, Esq., of Rochester.

TAUGHANNOCK FALLS—CAYUGA LAKE.

TRADITION CONCERNING THE ORIGIN OF THE NAME.

BY D. H. HAMILTON, D.D.

————•♦•————

IT is a curious question to the student of American antiquities, and especially of Indian archæology, how the Delaware name Taughannock came to be affixed to the most conspicuous and beautiful water-fall in the country of the Iroquois or Six Nations, and within the canton of the tribe of the Cayugas.

Did the ancient Delawares once hold this country, and did they then fix their name on these falls so firmly that the changes of war and conquest could not remove it, or was the name the result of some later event?

A faint tradition is in favor of the former supposition, but a more distinct one supports the latter.

3

Taughannock Falls is within the territory formerly owned by the Cayugas. Its name is accounted for, by history and tradition, in the following events.

The Iroquois confederacy, by a series of conquests, had extended its sway from Lake Superior and the Mississippi to Massachusetts Bay, and from Canada to the Potomac and Ohio. In fact, they held the Indians of almost the whole continent in subjection, and exacted of them tribute, which some of them pay to this day.

After subduing the Adirondacs, the Ottawas, the Chippewas, and the Algonkins, of the north; the Mohegans, the Manhattans, and the Nassachusets, on the east; the Cries, Miamies, and the Illini, on the west, and the Shawnees, on the Ohio, they con-quered also the Delawares, reduced them to "*Tichatains*," and took from them all authority in war or council, stigmatizing them as women. This took place at an early date. The Delawares were a powerful tribe situated on the Delaware and Susquehanna rivers, and in early times were formidable in the chase and on the war-path, and famed for their wisdom in the council. Of their many heroes, Tammany has left the proudest name.

Tammany, like Powhatan, was a great character at the time of the first coming of Europeans, and died at an advanced age in 1680.

Taghcanic, or Taughannock, or Taucahanac, was the name of a race of chieftains who ruled before the days of Tammany, and gave their name to several streams in the country where they lived. Some of these still remain as the names of branches of the Susquehanna and Delaware rivers.

They were supplanted in their chieftainship by Tammany and his successors, probably by some ancestor of the renowned Tammany, who has been canonized as St. Tammany, and is the presiding genius of so many halls, cabals, clubs, and political conclaves, especially of the well-known Tammany Hall, New-York.

The reign of the Tammanys seems to have been long, and was in the height of its ascendency, when they were overthrown by the more powerful Iroquois.

Falling before this mighty foe, they still retained their ancient pride; for Tammany made himself famous by his battles with the conquerors, and tradition states that he never had his equal in the chase or on the war-path.

While his people perished by the hand of the enemy, his own fame remained undimmed. ‚ Probably he is known further and honored more for the sad fate of his nation, so that their disaster was his glory.

After the Delawares had been conquered by the Six Nations, a controversy arose between the chiefs of the former tribe and the Governor of Pennsylvania, concerning the transfer of some lands at the forks of the Delaware. The whites appealed to the Iroquois, who decided that they had fairly purchased the lands in dispute, and sent Canassatego,* a chief of the Onondagas and a cotemporary of the great Logan, to inform the Delawares of their decision.

Canassatego appeared in Philadelphia with two hundred and thirty warriors. He told the Governor that the Delawares were in the wrong; that the Iroquois had long before subjugated them, and reduced them to the condition of women ; that they had no right whatever to say any thing about lands, or to appear in councils. Then, turning to

---

* For a full history of Canassatego, see Mr. Clark's " History of the County of Onondaga."

the Delaware chiefs present, he poured forth a
fierce torrent of invective against them and their
race, stigmatizing them as dishonest cowards, un-
worthy of the name of warriors, and therefore to
be known as *women*.

In conclusion, he commanded them to deliver up
to the whites the lands in dispute, which command
the unhappy Delawares, unable to resist, were constrained to obey.

The whole speech of Canassatego both to the
Governor of Pennsylvania and to the Delawares,
may be found in Colden's *Six Nations*, and in
Drake's *Book of Indians*, Book V., chap. 2.

The effect of this rebuke and taunt was overwhelming on the poor remnants of the once mighty
Delawares, and they shrank away and fled to the
interior to be lost in other tribes.

They had become, no doubt, dissipated, demoral-
ized, and wasted by their intercourse with the
whites, as well as humbled by the sway of the Six
Nations, or Mingoes, as they were called by the
Delawares, yet there was not wholly lost in that
poor tribe the "blood of noble breeding," nor the
spirit of the olden days.

A young chief of the ancient line of Taughannock was in that company, and every word of the sarcastic and reproachful speech of Canassatego, the proud Iroquois, stung him to the quick.

The shame of his race was a humiliation, and the haughty scorn of the Onondaga chief burnt into his soul. He vowed revenge, and collecting a few young warriors, they held a war-dance around the council-fire, and yelled their rage, and hurled their hatchets, and howled their vengeance, and enacted their mimic strategy—attack, grapple, slaughter, and victory, till the night was far gone. Then, filled with frenzy and panting with fiendish fury, they dashed forth on the war-path, nearly two hun· dred strong, and, traversing forest and mountain, crossing streams and gorges, made their way towards the canton of the Cayugas, intending a raid through the heart of the Iroquois country.

They passed Wyoming and Owego, and took the trail for Cayuga Lake, plotting to fall upon the Indian towns lying around it, especially *Neodakheat*, (Ithaca,) *Deowendote*, (Aurora,) and *Genogeh*, (Canoga.) Fearing, however, to attack Neodakheat, they turned to the left, and, pursuing their way northward, entered the Cayuga country lying between Cayuga and Seneca Lakes, meaning to make an attack on Genogeh, and then rush back and fall upon Neodakheat.

They encountered, however, an unexpected resistance from some smaller settlements of Indians situated in the regions where Trumansburgh, Perry, Mecklenburgh, Farmerville, and Lodi have since been located. These Indians were both Cayugas and Senecas; the chief settlement* of the former being between Perry and Mecklenburgh, while that of the Senecas was between Pratts and Farmerville. The two tribes were, however, much intermingled, and assumed a name indicative of their origin, calling themselves Ganungueuguch, that is, Sene-cayugas.

This union was brought about, for the most part, by an aspiring and talented young chief, whose father was a Seneca and whose mother was a Cayuga. The name of the chief and of the community—for they never rose to the full dignity of a tribe—was derived from Ganundesaga, (Seneca Lake,) and Gueuguch, (Cayuga Lake.) Ganungueuguch was

* Traces of this Indian settlement, together with an ancient fortification, may still be seen on the farm of Mr. Wm. Carman, near Perry City.

the Indian name of the chief, the settlements, the people, the stream, and of the Falls.

This chief gave his name to the river upon which he dwelt, just as Powhatan* left his name to the river and the country where he lived.

These two settlements, the one of Cayugas and the other of Senecas, consisting each of from four to six hundred souls, formed a very considerable community. They were made rich and happy by the abundance of game and of wild fruit, for which this region was famed among all the tribes.

On finding a hostile band of Delawares armed and painted for war passing through their immediate neighborhood, they took the alarm, rallied under their chief, Ganungueuguch, and made an ineffectual attempt to repel them.

The determined foe, however, after doing them some damage, pushed by them with little loss.

They sent messengers to *Genogeh*, the home of Red Jacket, and to *Deowendote*, and to *Neodakheat*,

* What a pity that the name Powhatan was ever abandoned for James River! And we can hardly withhold regret that the name Senecayuga, instead of Taughannock, was not retained for these falls!

informing their friends and allies that an enemy was in their land.

Before the Delawares arrived at Genogeh, word had been sent to Owasco, (now Auburn,) and to Onondaga, the home of Canassatego, informing him that his most bitter foes were on his track thirsting for revenge.

Starting from his security, and gathering a band of warriors around him, he hastened to Owasco and rallied a few more of his followers. Crossing the lake at Wasguas,* he arrived with his men at Genogeh, where the inhabitants had already been alarmed and were awaiting him in council.

Red Jacket,† then a mere lad, was there, Genogeh being his birthplace, and thus early became familiar with warlike councils, in which in after years he became so conspicuous as an orator.

At the head of at least two hundred braves, Canassatego marched from Genogeh southward and soon fell in with the enemy. There were frequent skirmishes, the Delawares always managing to keep

---

* The Indian name for the spot now called Cayuga Bridge.

† Red Jacket (whose Indian name was "Sa-go-ye-wat-ha," "He keeps them awake") was born near the famous spring of Canoga, in 1750.

a way open for retreat. Being followed all day,
they came at night to the stream which we have
seen bore the name of Ganungueuguch, or in English, Senecayuga, as indicating the fact that it
flowed through the territories of two tribes and was
in part named by both.

The Delawares pitched their night-camp, without
fire, between Perry and Waterburgh.   Here on the
morrow they found themselves confronted by a band
of the Neodakheats, (or Ithacans,) who were just
on the other side of the stream.   Immediately they
discovered the Ganungueuguch coming upon them
from the west.   At the same time the scouts of
Canassatego were approaching on the north.

Thus hemmed in, they had no retreat but toward
the lake.   Attempting this, Canassatego, by a sudden advance, anticipated them and marched up to
meet them on the left bank of the stream.

The Ganungueuguch pressed in from the west,
coming down on the left bank of the stream bearing the same name, while the Neodakheats were on
the opposite (or south) side.

The precise spot of the first encounter is unknown.   Doubtless the conflict raged along the left

bank, for perhaps a mile, from what is now Halsey-
ville to the falls.

The stream, being flooded by recent rains, could be
crossed with difficulty, and the Neodakheats, with
their arrows and war-clubs, were ready to defend
the other bank.

Coming at length to the gorge above the falls,
the unfortunate Delawares attempted to cross at the
place where W. B. Dumont's house now stands, but
they were again repulsed. Driven along the shore,
they pressed on toward the lake, feeling thankful
that the ever-deepening gorge, with its precipitous
rocks, defended them from one body of their foes.
Approaching the falls, they found their old foes,
whom they had supposed to be behind them, were
now in their front prepared to give them battle.

Here, then, took place the last encounter.

The young Taughannock and his band determined to sell their lives as dear as possible. Death
in some form was inevitable, and they resolved to
meet it like warriors.

In the encounter, Taughannock, striking down
Ganunguenguch, sought to close with Canassatego
himself. Breaking through the circle of braves
which surrounded him, he precipitated himself,

knife in hand, upon his deadly foe. He inflicted several mortal wounds before he was finally overpowered and struck down by the attendants of the chief.

Tradition tells us that his bleeding but not yet lifeless body was thrown over the precipice into the depths below the falls, and that most of his band shared his fate. But few escaped. Some were taken and tortured. Two, who were strong and well-favored, were adopted by the Cayugas, who had lost friends in the battle.

The more common version is, that Taughannock, after he was overpowered, was reserved for torture, and thus perished on the brink of the falls ; that the Ganunguenguch, into whose country he had made his incursion, and whose chief he had killed, and especially the followers of Canassatego, on whom he had sought and taken revenge, engaged in the torture with unusual delight. That Taughannock sang his death-song, defied his enemies, rejoiced that he had killed so many of the foes of his nation, hurled back defiance at his tormentors, and died with a bravery as savage as was the ferocity of his torturers. That when dead, his remains were not honored by being consumed by fire, as was usual, but were thrown over the precipice, to be devoured by wild beasts or waste away unburied.

Be these things as they may, thus came the Delaware name Taughannock to be affixed to the falls within the region of the Cayugas, and to supersede that of Ganungueuguch, or, in English, Senecayuga, which originally and more appropriately belonged to them.

Nor is this derivation, or the history of this name, more strange than the manner in which Greek names were carried all over Asia and the East, by the expeditions of Alexander; and the way in which the Latin language was extended by the Romans over Western Europe, and even England.

Taughannock fell, but his name lives in the falls, the most beautiful object in the country of his enemies, where he died to wipe out the disgrace of his nation's defeat and shame, and to avenge his own personal wrongs.

Such is fame, whether in civilized or savage life. It is the cost of blood or toil that for the time seems to fall fruitless to the ground, but lives in after times, springing up and bearing the laurels of imperishable memories.

GEOLOGY OF TAUGHANNOCK.

THE following account of the geological features of the ravines at Taughannock, has been carefully compiled from several volumes of geological surveys, but principally from the large work which forms Volume IV. of the *Natural History of the State*, which contains a very full and accurate account, by Professor Hall, of the formation of the Fourth Geological District, in which he treats at length of the structure of the rocks at Taughannock, and gives an engraving of the fall.

The descriptions of the various formations are given nearly in the words of Professor Hall; and while they are peculiarly valuable to the student of geology, they will be found interesting and instructive to all.

It will be noticed that Taughannock affords a remarkable example of the power of comparatively small bodies of water to make vast excavations in the solid rock.

GEOLOGICAL ACCOUNT.

Taughannock, the highest perpendicular fall of water in the State, is one of the numerous cataracts of the Portage group. The upper part of the group, being composed of sandstone of a much harder nature than the lower part, produces cliffs and waterfalls in all the streams passing over it. Nowhere else do we meet with more beautiful cascades or more grand and striking scenery. The pedestrian often finds his course impeded by a gorge of several hundred feet in depth; and in the very bottom of this, now scarcely perceptible, is the winding stream—the only representative of the once powerful torrent that has excavated the deep channel. Farther on, above or below, he may see the little stream dashed over a precipice, and almost disappearing in spray before it reaches the bottom; here, however, it gathers itself in a deep pool, from which it flows on quietly as before, or gurgling and dashing through the fragments of the fallen cliffs, finds its way into the gently sloping valley of the softer shales.

At Taughannock an immense chasm is formed into which the water descends perpendicularly two hundred and fifteen feet, from the bottom of which we see the amphitheatre of rocks rising around us, and, by the effect of perspective, closing over our heads.

The black shale, visible for eighty feet above the Tully limestone, is succeeded by more than two hundred feet of the next series, consisting in the lower part of a mass of silicious shale, and above alternating with argillaceous sandstone.

The surfaces of this rock are often rippled, and covered with minute fragments of vegetables, which seem to follow the course of the marking, and accumulate or diminish with the ripple wave. The same appearance is presented by a beach of sand, where the ebbing tide leaves fine fragments of vegetable matter, arranged in quantity and direction proportionate to the wave.

One can almost fancy himself still upon the shore of some quiet bay or arm of the sea, where the waves of the receding tide have left these little ridges of sand, which on their return will be obliterated and mingled with the mass around. The shells and fragments and the clouded sand all lie around him with a freshness of appearance that might almost make him doubt. But his foot is upon the firm rock, and his hand can not obliterate the faint wave-lines, nor remove a single shell from its place.

Every thing is firm and fixed, and he is forced to recollect that millions of ages have rolled on since this shore was washed by the sea.

How beautiful, how simple and grand is this exhibition! and how much does it illumine the mind as to the mode of production of these older formations which have been considered so obscure.

Here was an ocean, supplied with all the materials for forming rocky strata; in its deeper parts were going on the finer depositions, and on its shores were produced the sandy beaches and the pebbly banks. All, for aught we know, was as bright and beautiful as upon our ocean shores of the present day; the tide ebbed and flowed, its waters ruffled by the gentle breeze, and nature wrought in all her various forms as at the present time, though man was not there to say, How beautiful!

Although the rocks of this group have a thickness of one thousand feet or more, still they contain few fossils, and may be examined in many localities without discovering any. Indeed, unless very strict

3*

search were made, one would be likely to pronounce them non-fossiliferous.

In general character, the fossils differ essentially from those below.

The Tully limestone and shale below disappear in Cayuga Lake, four miles below Ithaca, the black shale extending about two miles further south.

These layers of sandstone furnish the finest flag-stones in the country, being of any required thickness, often twenty feet in length, and five to ten in width.

The numerous and picturesque waterfalls of the western part of the State are intimately connected with the modern action of rivers and streams in ex-cavating and deepening their channels. That every fall of water is receding by wearing back its bed will admit of demonstrative proof, wherever obser-vations have been continued for any length of time. Even the short period of four or five years has been sufficient to show, in many instances, a con-stant, gradual recession, varying with the quantity of water and the nature of the rock. The greatest amount of water does not always, however, appear to be attended with the most rapid recession; for where the stream is so small as to be entirely frozen during winter, the effects of ice on the strata seem even more efficient than the wearing of water.

The loosening of masses near the edge, at least, enables the water afterward to remove them with greater facility.

Where we find these falls upon streams half a mile from their junction with a large lake, it is difficult to conceive how they have once commenced their operations on its margin, and we are readily disposed to admit any hypothesis that will account for the previous excavation of a lateral valley to this distance from the main one. Where these channels expand rapidly toward their outlets, and slope gradually upward, it seems a fair inference that some agency other than the wearing of the stream has had a share in producing its present condition ; but where we find a regular chasm, with perpendicular and nearly parallel sides, with a fall of water at its extremity, we are compelled, from all analogy, to admit that the stream has been the agent producing it.

At Taughannock, there seems originally to have been a broad, shallow depression, in which the stream commenced flowing toward the lake.

In its passage, it first produced a series of falls

and rapids, but finally receded so as to form but a single fall. This is caused by the higher strata being so much harder than those below that a firm table is formed of these, while those beneath are undermined.

Although there may have been originally an indentation at this point from the valley of Cayuga Lake, yet there seems conclusive evidence that the stream has been the chief agent in producing this immense chasm.

The numerous seams freely admit the water, which during winter is frozen, and thus from the whole face of the cliff immense quantities are detached. In this way the upper portion is left projecting beyond the lower till it is broken off.

The first process is constant; and immense masses of fragments, some scarcely less than fifty tons, may be seen, which have fallen down.

The lower of the two more prominent arenaceous strata, about half way up the cliff, is the one presenting the fine casts of striæ, alluded to in the description of these under Portage group. (Nat. Hist. N. Y., Part IV. p. 336.)

Beautiful specimens may be obtained at this

place after the falling of a mass, or by approaching the stratum at some accessible point.

Many of the strata in the channel of the stream
above the fall present these casts in great perfection.

POETRY OF TAUGHANNOCK.

"Why on NIAGARA lavish all your lays?
Come, heavenly Muse, and sing TAUGHANNOCK's praise."

SONG OF THE WATERFALL.

BY MATTIE WINFIELD TORREY.

IN the gloom and shade of the forest deep,
Where the rocks lie piled in a frowning steep,
Where the sun comes rarely nor lingers long,
The waterfall chanteth its ceaseless song.

"I come, I come! from my rocky bed,
Through the densest shade of the forest led;
'Neath the trailing boughs that are bending low,
And the tangled grasses swift I go.

"I rush through the caves where the shadows sleep,
I glide o'er the pools that lie still and deep,
I sparkle and dance in the sunlight gay,
And murmur a song to beguile my way.

"I come, I come! from the mountain height
Where the sun rests warm as he sinks at night,

From the dewy mead and the flow'ry burn,
I come, I come! but I ne'er return.

"In the sounding depths of this forest dim,
Whose arches reëcho my ceaseless hymn,
I leap with a glad, an exultant song,
O'er the fatal verge I have sought so long.

"The dizzying whirl of the blinding spray
Enshrouds me quite as I hasten away,
'Neath the frowning banks that are high and steep,
Till I lose myself in the lake so deep."

The rays of the sun came shivering through,
And the silvery vapors were curled anew,   ·
While the tide formed many a snowy wreath,
Ere it broke in foam on the rocks beneath.

And the headlong plunge of the ceaseless tide
As it madly leaped down the chasm wide,
With its endless din and its busy strife,
Methought was an image of human life.

TAUGHANNOCK—THE RIVER AND FALL.

BY LEWIS HALSEY.

I.

Rippling and flashing, now,
Foaming and splashing, now,
Wanders the streamlet, its banks bright with flowers;

Skipping so merrily,
Singing so cheerily,
Lingers 'mid Nature's most beautiful bowers.

II.

Gleaming and glimmering,
   Shining and shimmering,
Glowing with purity, splendor, and light;
   Now sinking fearfully,
   Sadly, and tearfully,
Into the depths of the gathering night.

III.

   Dark cliffs are covering,
   Shadows are hovering
Over the shivering streamlet below;
   Terror soon banishing,
   Dangers all vanishing,
Soon it subsides to its usual flow.

IV.

   Eddying pettishly,
   Smiling coquettishly;
Now its waves rise again only to sink;
   Sportively wandering,
   Seemingly pondering
Whether to leap o'er the terrible brink.

v.

Shifting and shivering,
Quaking and quivering,
Glides the sad stream o'er the horrible steep;
No murmur muttering,
Foamy wings fluttering,
Sinking in mists to the darkening deep.

vi.

Oft we are wondering,
Blind in our blundering,
Whence is thy power to charm and delight?
Still thou art haunting us,
Ever enchanting us,
Vision of beauty which bursts on our sight!

vii.

Emblem of purity,
Through all futurity,
While upon mortals thy beauties shall shine,
Making us lowlier,
Humbler, and holier,
Nature's true worshipers ever are thine!

From Moore's Rural New-Yorker.

TO TAUGHANNOCK.

BY H.

BRIGHT visions—thoughts of beauty and of song,
Come to my mind unbidden; as I view

Thy gentle flow, thy silvery spray, thy rocks
Majestic, and thy far extending chasm,
Riven broad and deep by Nature's mighty hand.
How many years have passed away, since first
Thy waters gave this steep majestic plunge,
No tongue can tell, no history can show.
Perhaps since first Creation's hand attired
The dark and formless earth, and bade the streams,
The rivulets, to spring from mountain sides
To wander through the valleys to the sea,
These rocks and woods have echoed mournfully
Thy ceaseless roar, thy spirit-stirring song.
May no rude hand mar thy wild loveliness!
But let the hearts of those, who, ages hence,
Shall gaze upon thy wondrous sheeted form,
Feel awe as deep, and reverential love,
As did the wild untutored forest child,
When he beheld, with mingled love and fear,
Thy beauty-clad majestic cataract;
And well he loved to watch thy ceaseless flow,
And hear thy never silent thunder tones—
Reclining 'neath the leafy forest's shade,
And turning oft to view the pleasant shores
Of bright Cayuga, which he loved to call
His happy hunting-grounds.

ODE TO TAUGHANNOCK.

BY LIDA MEDDIC.

POETS have sung in rapturous numbers
Of numerous famed cataracts over the world,
But the Muses, methinks, are deep in their slumbers,
If *thy* "cadenced white waterfall silvered and curled,"
Does not make them to sing, with a heart all aglow,
Of the beauty above and the beauty below.

With eyes far too dreamy for aught save thy beauty,
I see the white column of watery snow,
So slowly descending and ceaseless in duty,
To join the swift rushing of wavelets below,
That, by a charmed circle of silvery mist,
Ever rising and falling, so often are kissed.

I hear thy grand voice in melodious anthem,
Resound with the praises of "God and the free,"
Amid the dim arches, and echo on echo
Shall ever be heard by the evergreen tree,
Of a song that is endless, a song that is true,
Of a spirit that fosters the "red, white, and blue."

O sweet lovely scene! for the high and the lowly,
Thy phases so wondrous are made to exist;
Blessed boon! to view the face of the Holy,
In the hues of the rainbow or forms of the mist,
Mixed with things of earth in compounds so rare,
That with heaven and angels we seek to compare.

Imagery paints with warm, busy fingers,
A picture for hope that vies with the past,
And memory points, as the vision still lingers,
To dreams far too bright and too lovely to last;
But thy name, dear Taughannock, shall never decay,
And thy beauty grow brighter, as time wears away!

From the Ithaca Citizen and Democrat.

EXTRACT FROM BOTANIZING.

A REMINISCENCE OF 1862.

BY L. L.

.   .   .   .

Soon, the narrow ledge behind them,
They approach the great Taughannock:
Hear the roaring of its waters,
Like the sound of many thunders:
See the sparkling foam-clouds waving,
Like a vail of misty whiteness:
See the mighty walls of granite,
Towering upward, towering upward:
See the waters leaping, dashing
From the lofty ledge above them.
Thoughts of grandeur and of beauty
Fill each heart to overflowing,
For the thunder of the waters
Has a power like that of music,
Breathes a fairy spell around them,
Sends a thrill to every bosom.

Filled with awe, they gaze delighted,
And a still voice speaks within them—
A small voice speaks gently to them—
Low in tone but full of power:
　" Glorious art thou, O Taughannock !
　　In thy majesty and beauty,
　　In thy wondrous weight of waters,
　　In thy towering walls of granite,
　　In thy ceaseless, wild commotion,
　　In thy vail so white and misty,
　　In thy rainbow-sparkling foam-cloud,
　　In thy sweet, eternal music !"

TAUGHANIC FALLS.

BY REV. HENRY PARKER.

I.

Ye bards and travelers ! Oh ! talk no more
　Of Scotland's misty crags, and linns, and lakes,
Nor tell us how the waters at Lodore
　Come down, nor how the Rhine in fury breaks,
Nor how, at Reichenbach, the torrents pour,
　And all the solid ground at Staubbach shakes :
I care no more for these, nor sigh to see
The Falls of Terni and of Tivoli.

II.

I've read enough of these, and seen Niagara,
　Which is the king of cataracts forever,

And it is certainly a sight to stagger a
    Poor poet's or a painter's best endeavor ;
And other falls I've seen, but such a crag or a
    Remarkable cascade, beheld I never,
As that which gave me quite a poet's panic,
When late I gazed upon our own Taughanic.
    .   .   .   .

III.

Roll on, Taughanic's wild and shouting stream,
    Here darkly winding in thy gloomy deeps,
And there reflecting back the sunny gleam
    That slants athwart the cliffs and dizzy steeps.
As wild and varied thou, as is the dream
    That hovers o'er the couch where beauty sleeps—
As wild and fearless thou, as those whose claim
To this our land first gave to thee thy name.

IV.

'Tis sweet to look on thee when summer's morn
    Hath touched thy lordly battlements with gold,
And when the mists, that of the night are born,
    In rosy wreaths and clouds are upward rolled ;
'Tis sweet to see thy walls, with ruin worn,
    O'erhung with fragrant pines and gray with mould,
All silvered with the moonbeams, cold and white,
Or blushing in the torches' ruddy light.

V.

Thine amphitheatre, ascending wide,
    Calls up a vision of the storied past—

The chariots coursing swiftly, side by side,
   Within the Coliseum's circle vast,
The gladiator who in silence died,
   The shower of garlands on the victor cast,
The deadly stroke—the shout—the cruel throng—
I gladly turn from thoughts of death and wrong.

VI.

I love to think that in thy rocky walls,
   Where stands the strangely perfect Gothic Door,
The genii have reared their magic halls,
   With crystal column and with pearly floor,
And fountains, where the tinkling water falls,
   And arching roof, with jewels studded o'er—
A mystic realm in secret silence bound,
Until the spell to open it is found.

VII.

I love to think that flitting fay and elf
   Are hidden in thy darkling nooks and dells,
Or that, beneath the cascade's jutting shelf
   A spirit, matchless in her beauty, dwells,
And wraps these misty robes about herself,
   And ever sings, and weaves her wondrous spells,
Until revealed at some fond dreamer's call—
The lovely Undine of the waterfall.

TAUGHANNOCK HOUSE,

TAUGHANNOCK FALLS,

J. S. HALSEY, Proprietor.

———•••———

THIS favorite Hotel, having been this season enlarged, refitted, and refurnished, is now open for the accommodation of visitors.

All that can make a hotel attractive and interesting to tourists or pleasure-parties may here be found.

The Taughannock House is situated just opposite the Falls, two and one half miles from the village of TRUMANSBURGH, and ten miles from ITHACA.

Cayuga Lake boats, touching four times per day at the landing near the Falls, connect with the New-York Central and the New-York and Erie Railroads. A carriage will be in readiness at the landing to convey visitors to the hotel.

The far-famed Cayuga offers ample accommodation to the sportsman for FISHING and BOATING.

Being off from the line of *direct* communication with the Atlantic cities, near the banks of the beautiful Cayuga, surrounded by a pure, clear, and bracing atmosphere, it presents peculiar inducements to travelers in search of a healthful summer residence.

Particular attention will be given to orders for rooms during the summer.   Address,

J. S. HALSEY,
Trumansburgh, New-York.